JUNGLE DOCTOR'S HIPPO HAPPENINGS

④

JUNGLE DOCTOR'S HIPPO HAPPENINGS

Paul White

CF4·K

10 9 8 7 6 5 4 3 2 1

Jungle Doctor's Hippo Happenings

ISBN 978-1-84550-611-7

© Copyright 1966 Paul White

First published 1966. Second impression 1970

Paperback edition 1972. Reprinted twice. New edition 1983

Reprinted 1985, 1987, 1988, 1989,1997

Published in 2010 by

Christian Focus Publications, Geanies House, Fearn, Tain,

Ross-shire, IV20 1TW, Scotland, U.K.

Paul White Productions,

4/1-5 Busaco Road, Marsfield, NSW 2122, Australia

Cover design: Daniel van Straaten

Cover illustration: Craig Howarth

Interior illustrations: Graham Wade

Printed and bound by Bell and Bain, Glasgow

Mixed Sources

Product group from well-managed
forests and other controlled sources
www.fsc.org Cert no. TT-COC-002769
© 1996 Forest Stewardship Council

FSC

Scripture quotations are either the author's own paraphrase
or are taken from The New Testament in Modern English,
copyright © 1958, 1959, 1960
J.B. Phillips and 1947, 1952, 1955, 1957
The Macmillian Company, New York.
Used by permission. All rights reserved.

CONTENTS

INTRODUCTION

Paul White learned a great deal from his African friends at the jungle hospital. They befriended him and helped him in his efforts to learn their language, Chigogo.

One of their most important gifts was to teach him how to use animal stories. These stories, or fables, helped to explain abstract thoughts and theological terms.

When the Whites were on their way home from Africa in 1941, they were delayed in Colombo because of German submarine activity. Paul was invited to speak at a girls' boarding school. All the children of non-Christian faiths were sent outside but, hearing laughter from inside, crowded round the windows to see what they were missing. This was the first of many occasions when audiences were gripped by the fable stories.

The first of six fable books appeared in 1955. A menagerie of African animals is used to teach the gospel and how to live the Christian life. In these books you will meet Toto, the mischievous monkey, Boohoo, the hippo who, like the author, suffered from allergies, Twiga, the giraffe and wise teacher, and many others.

They will endear themselves to you as they have to thousands round the globe.

PROLOGUE

Daudi shook his head as he looked through the hospital window at the eager faces below him.

'Not tonight. Would you have me tell stories when a great trouble has struck our part of East Africa?'

'What trouble, Great One?'

'It is called smallpox, a disease of no joy whatsoever. It scars the skin. Often it blinds people, and sometimes it kills. We are preparing to fight it with a special treatment which protects from its attack.'

Gogo, who stood behind Tali and Kali, the twins, said, 'Cannot we help?'

'Tell us about it and we will tell others,' said Elizabeti, the schoolmaster's daughter.

Jungle Doctor's voice came over Daudi's shoulder, 'Daudi, these young friends of ours could be very useful in what we're planning to do. Why not tell them all about it and ...' He dropped his voice.

Daudi smiled and nodded. 'Listen, everybody, all of you be under the *buyu* tree at the time of sunsetting. Tonight there will be no story, but you will see something that will make your eyes open wide. And remember, we need your help very much. Oh, Goha, the Bwana wants you to come now and be vaccinated with the helpers of the hospital.'

'What's vaccinated mean?' asked Yuditi.

'I'll tell you under the *buyu* tree,' laughed Daudi.

In the late afternoon the children were in an excited group. Goha came up to them. '*Hongo*, there is nothing to fear.'

'*Heeh!*' said Elizabeti, 'I do not like needles being stuck into me.'

'*Koh*,' sniffed Goha, 'this doesn't hurt. Anyhow they don't stick needles into you at all. They only scratch the skin a v-e-r-y little.'

'How do you know these things?' asked Dan.

'Did I not watch your father and the doctor vaccinate the helpers at the hospital? Have I not been done also?'

'Where?' demanded Yuditi.

Goha rolled up his sleeve.

'*Koh*, I can't see anything.'

'I told you it was a small thing,' said Goha.

'*Hongo!*' cried Elizabeti, 'see, they come now, Bwana Daudi and the doctor.'

A moment later Jungle Doctor unwrapped a towel and spread it on the biggest root of the *buyu* tree. 'Everybody, I want you to watch with careful eyes so that you may understand and talk with knowledge. Goha, today you have seen the way we vaccinate people?'

'*Eheh*, Bwana. I have been telling my friends that it is a small thing and nothing to fear.'

'You speak words of truth, and to prove it, do you think you could vaccinate me?'

The boy's eyes nearly popped out. '*Eheh*, Bwana, I could do it, if you'd let me.'

Jungle Doctor smiled. 'I want you to.'

Goha hurried to the hospital to wash his hands. Panting he returned and took from the towel a tiny glass tube containing some milky fluid. He broke both ends off, picked up a moist swab, rubbed the doctor's arm and then let a drop of the fluid from the tube fall a few inches below the shoulder. Then with a needle he pricked the skin three times lightly.

'Did it hurt, Bwana?' asked Yuditi.

'No, not even a little.'

Goha put down the needle. 'The work is finished, Bwana.'

'*Eheh*,' said Daudi, 'and that is all that needs to be done to pull out the teeth and cut off the claws of this fierce sickness that can spread like a bush fire.'

'Bwana,' said Gogo, 'do me now.'

'Do us all!' cried Elizabeti.

11

When everyone had been vaccinated they stood looking at one another and smiling. Kali asked, 'Has nothing else to be done?'

'Nothing, and what will happen is in five days there will be red swelling or a blister the size of your thumbnail. This will quickly heal, and within your blood will be the strength to defend you from this vicious illness.'

'Bwana,' said Tali, 'we can go round to the homes of our friends here and in other villages and tell people how simple it all is.'

'Do this, and you will save many people's lives.'

'We shall come here tomorrow at the same time, Bwana, and bring you news of our talking.'

'Good,' said Daudi, 'and I will have a hippo story to tell you.'

'*Yoh!*' laughed Gogo, 'wouldn't it be a tough job to vaccinate a hippopotamus!'

1
THE HELPFULNESS OF HIPPO

There was a lot of excited chatter under the buyu tree at sundown next evening. At first Goha and Gogo had arrived wheeling Gulu, whose leg was in plaster, in the hospital wheelbarrow. More slowly behind came Elizabeti and Yuditi, between them a small girl both of whose eyes were bandaged.

Yuditi said, 'Bwana Daudi will come soon, Liso. He tells wonderful stories.'

'Eheh,' said Elizabeti, 'and we have good news for him. Have not many people listened to our words and looked at the places where we were vaccinated, and are they not coming tomorrow to the hospital?'

'Many have already come,' said Tali and Kali, the twins. 'That is why Bwana Daudi has not yet appeared.'

'Here he comes now,' said Gogo.

Daudi smiled at them. 'Yoh!' he said, 'I have been busy springing the trap of this disease, smallpox. Truly vaccination is an excellent way of doing this. But look in here.' He held out a cardboard box.

'What is it?' whispered Liso.

Goha's voice answered, 'Koh! A loop of strong wire. A snare for animals?'

'Eheh,' said Daudi. 'They are evil things. If ever you come across one remove it with care, and remember, the great expert in setting traps is ... '

'Shaitan, the devil!' muttered Gogo.

'Hongo!' Gulu looked at his plaster-covered leg. 'I should hate to be caught in one of those.'

Daudi nodded. 'All traps take away your freedom and bring no joy. Those of small wisdom walk into them with their eyes wide open, but everybody at some time falls into one certain trap – the deadliest of the whole lot.'

'You speak of the sin trap, Bwana Daudi?'

'I do indeed. And how do you get into it?'

'By doing things that are wrong and not doing things that you know to be right,' answered Goha.

'And can you get out by yourself?'

'No,' came the chorus of voices.

Daudi leaned back against the trunk of the great tree and said:

In the thicker parts of the jungle Mwoko, the hunter's son threw down a great load of dry grass beside a deep dark hole that gaped in the path. 'A trap of value this,' said Hunter, as he skilfully spread the grass over a frame of light sticks. 'The sides slope like the neck of a great gourd – those that fall in won't get out. Tomorrow at the heat of noon when no feet move through the jungle but yours and mine, Mwoko, we shall return and find meat for our cooking-pot or skins to sell in the marketplace. Truly there is profit in this great trap.'

Even as they were talking, Dic-Dic, the antelope, came trotting along the river bank. Boohoo, the hippo, snoozed blissfully in his favourite water-lily pond. Dic-Dic stood looking at the large round nostrils, which were just above water level.

A sudden mischievous idea raced through his mind. He ran off to the jungle and found a tree covered with little yellow ball-like flowers. He broke a piece off and tip-hooved back. As quietly as he could he came close to Boohoo holding the branch with the yellow flowers between his teeth. He shook his head gently and a cloud of pollen settled on Hippo's nose.

A ripple spread across the pond, then a bigger one. Boohoo's eyes opened. His nose twitched. 'Oh dear! I'b going to ... I'b going to ... sneeze!'

'I thought you would,' chuckled Dic-Dic.

Hippo sneezed in a way that shook all the nearby trees. He lurched out of the pond and stood looking hard at Dic-Dic.

'*Er* – that wasn't funny. I'b going to – *um* – bite you!'

Dic-Dic bolted, leaping over bushes, bounding over anthills, chortling away to himself, 'Fancy him trying to catch me!'

He looked back over his shoulder and saw Boohoo lumbering along in the distance.

Ahead was a large and interesting-looking shadow. With a bound Dic-Dic landed neatly in the middle of it. A cloud of leaves and dry grass hit him in the face and he went head over hooves deep down into the darkness.

When his breath came back he found there was mud all round him and all he could see, through a ragged hole above him, was a patch of blue sky.

He tried to climb, but the walls were too steep. He tried to jump, but the mud held him down. He struggled frantically, but it was no good. He was caught. His only hope was in the light above him, and suddenly that too disappeared.

As he looked with terrified eyes he saw two round things that moved slowly about. He crouched in a corner hardly daring to breathe, and his heart nearly stopped beating when from between the round things came an eerie, echoing sound.

'*Er* – *um* – are you down there, Dic-Dic?'

Antelope's voice was squeaky with relief. 'Boohoo! I'm sorry ... '

'Never mind, Dic-Dic. I just wanted to teach you a lesson. But I never thought you would fall into this trap. *Er* – wait a minute!'

For a moment the light came back and Dic-Dic heard, 'Oh, Rhino, Antelope's fallen into the trap down there.'

'Stupid little beast,' ground out Rhino. 'Ought to have more sense. Ought to look where he's going. Tell him to watch his step in future, and to get out of there fast. I've seen Hunter's footprints all over the jungle today. When he comes back that will be the end of anybody in that trap.'

'*Oh – er* – no, I mean yes,' agreed Boohoo. 'Dic-Dic, Rhino says you're to watch your step in future. But don't worry. I'll work out some rules to help you not to fall into traps. *Er* – point … one …'

'But I'm IN this trap!' cried Dic-Dic. 'It's awful down here. There are things that … '

'Probably snakes,' said Boohoo. 'The worst sort live in the dark. *Er* – firstly, you must look out for places that are just covered over with leaves. Now, point two. Never walk on these. They are … what's the word? Ah, in-sub-stan-tial.'

Dic-Dic whispered, 'Will the hunter come soon?'

'Prob-ably. *Er* – what did you say, Rhino? *Oh – er* – that's a worrying thought. He says at midday, Dic-Dic. It just shows how careful you need to be with traps. Point three … '

'Boohoo, I want to get out. I want to get out NOW, before the hunter … '

A cheerful voice interrupted. 'What's going on here, Boohoo? What are you counting your toes for?'

'*Er* – that's one, two, three. Yes, I know, but Dic-Dic's in the trap. I'm helping him.'

'Helping him? How?'

'Well, you see, I – *er* – I've told him how danger-ous it is to fall into traps. I'm making some rules ...'

'That won't help him to get out! Dic-Dic, are you down there? It's Waddle, the duckling, here!'

There was a flutter of feathers and a small duck perched on the very edge of the trap and peered in. 'It's dark down there,' he quacked. 'More the place for snakes than worms. Pity you hadn't wings like mine. You could flap them, and *whoosh!* You'd be out.'

'But,' came Dic-Dic's small frightened voice, 'I haven't any wings, and I can't grow any!'

'Keep calm, Dic-Dic,' boomed Boohoo's voice. 'Thinking is very important. Say to yourself very con-vin-cing-ly, "There are no such things as traps".'

Antelope shivered and wondered what Boohoo meant.

Monkey scuttled over to the top of the trap and looked down. 'Cheer up, Dic-Dic, keep your wits about you, and you'll get out by yourself!'

He sounded so cheerful and confident that Dic-Dic found his spirits rising.

'Look around for something to stand on, then dig yourself steps with your paws, and climb out. It's simple!'

But as Dic-Dic nosed around in the gloom he found nothing. He tried to dig with his hooves, but it was no good. As his hopes faded he thought, 'It must be easier to dig with paws than with these things that I have at the end of my feet.'

The more he struggled, the more his spirits sank. There was no way out.

But Monkey had had another idea. He shot up a tree, broke off a stick, and was back in a flash.

'Dic-Dic,' he called, 'leave it to Monkey, and you'll be out in a jiffy.'

He poked the stick down into the darkness. Antelope stretched up his neck and was just able to grip it with his teeth. Toto's paws clutched the other end, but there was not room enough for him to hold it firmly.

Hyena, who, with Vulture, had been watching everything that happened from the shadows, laughed nastily. 'Monkey wisdom's a bit short, eh?'

Vulture made strange noises in his long scrawny neck, and started to sharpen his beak.

Boohoo brought his nose close to the hole in the leaves. 'Dic-Dic, I've thought out three, that is to say, four, ways of not – *um* – falling into traps. Now you know about them you'll find them very valu-able, I'm sure.'

Vulture looked at Hyena, and they both smirked, but Dic-Dic called with a small voice, 'Boohoo, is it nearly midday?'

Monkey was busily climbing the tree again chortling, 'Bigger, better sticks; that's the answer. Now we'll have him out before you can say COCONUT!' He came rushing to the side of the trap again with a long stick which was so thick that he could barely grip it between his paws. 'This one's plenty long enough,' he told Boohoo, 'and it won't break either.'

'*Er* – very sub-stan-tial,' murmured Hippo.

But Monkey was peering down into the darkness. 'Dic-Dic, here's another stick. A long strong one. Grab hold, and we'll have you out in no time.'

But Dic-Dic found it was too thick to grip properly with his teeth.

'Wind your tail around it!' yelled Monkey, 'and whatever you do, hang on!'

Boohoo ambled over to where Monkey was working busily. He put his chin under the end of the stick and slowly placed his front foot on top of it. '*Um* – sub-stan-tial stick this.'

'Are you all right?' shouted Monkey excitedly.

Dic-Dic could say nothing. His mouth was tightly closed around the stick.

'I have my foot in the right pos-i-tion now,' came Boohoo's voice. 'This will fix it.' He pushed hard. Down shot his end of the stick. Up rocketed the other.

Dic-Dic's neck jerked upwards. His head hit the top of the trap with a bang, and his teeth lost their grip. He fell back heavily – *Splash!* – into the mud.

'What happened?' shouted Monkey. 'Are you all right? Why didn't you hang on?'

Dic-Dic was dizzy with pain and disappointment.

'*Er* – I did my bit, you know,' said Hippo proudly. 'full of ass-i-s – *er* – ass-ist – *er* – that is, you'll always find me very helpful.'

Bruised and battered, Dic-Dic struggled to his feet. The fear in his heart grew. He'd never get out of this dreadful trap. He could see the sun now. It would soon be midday.

Another vulture arrived. Hyena licked his lips. Boohoo shook his head sadly. 'A pity. A very great pity. I'm sure we could have – *er* – worked out something if there had only been the opp – oppor – *um* – if we'd had much more time.'

Monkey sat scratching his head and making important agitated noises.

A great shadow moved silently through the trees and stopped near the edge of the trap. The vultures rose heavily into the air, and Hyena slunk away into the shadows. Dic-Dic's mouth went dry as the ground above him trembled with the movement of many feet.

He shuddered. Had the hunter arrived?

He shrank back in alarm as a long snake-like thing came over the edge of the trap.

'Dic-Dic, come over into the light!' It was a deep, friendly voice, and a wave of relief came into small Antelope's mind.

'Is it really you, Tembo?'

'Of course it is. Come over here where I can help you. This is your only way out.'

'But I've tried and tried, and I'm still trapped. And the others have tried too.'

There came the urgent whirr of Waddle's wings.

'Hurry!' he quacked, 'the hunter's very close now!'

'Trust me,' said Elephant quietly, 'leave it to me. Put your feet as high as you can.'

'But I'm not much good at holding on to things,' panted small Antelope.

'You don't have to. I'll hold you.'

Dic-Dic struggled on to his hind legs. He could see Elephant's trunk well within reach now, but inside his mind were all sorts of questions and doubts. 'Trust yourself to me,' came the comforting voice.

Dic-Dic put his legs on the curve of the trunk and felt it strong, holding him gently, but very firmly. All at once he felt a change come inside him. Tembo had said he could do it, and the strength of his grip gave the same message.

'Don't look back. Don't look down. Keep your eyes on me,' said Elephant.

Dic-Dic found himself being lifted out of the darkness. He felt his feet touch solid ground. He looked around. He was safe. His eyes said 'Thank you' far louder than his tongue ever could.

Elephant's words came clearly, 'Come with me. Let's go out of here together. And the closer you keep the safer you'll be.'

The small girl with the bandaged eyes put her hands out to Daudi, 'Great One, I'm in the sin trap. Oh, I know I am. Who is able to help me?'

'God's Son, Jesus, is the only One who can help,' said Daudi gently. 'If you ask him to forgive you, He will lift you out of the sin trap and show you, through the Bible, the way to live.'

There was a catch in the small girl's voice. 'If the medicines don't work on my eyes, I won't ever be able to read the Bible. I will never know.'

Daudi looked up. Elizabeti nodded. 'We will help you and read it to you.'

'Ngheeh!' said Daudi, 'that's the best way to take the deadliness out of traps, and it is very different from the helpfulness of hippos.'

* * *

What's Inside the Fable?

Special Message: Jesus will lift you out of your sin trap, if you ask him to.

Read *Psalm 40:1-4*

Read *1 John 1:8-10*

24

2

REFLECTIONS OF HIPPO

Gogo sat with his chin in his hand, 'How do you know all these things about smallpox, Bwana Doctor?'

'Books, Gogo. Look at this one. It tells all about the disease; how it starts, what causes it, the trouble it makes for your skin, your eyes, your life.'

'Where's the Bwana?' came Tali's frightened voice.

He dashed through the gate and came panting to the door. 'Quickly, Bwana, Kali has swallowed a bone and it chokes him!'

A crowd of hurrying figures was coming up the hill. In front was Baruti carrying Kali. Jungle Doctor hurried to the operating theatre, picked out some forceps and a surgical mirror with a handle.

Baruti was at the door. 'Hodi, Bwana?'

'Karibu, come in, Baruti. Bring him over here. Lie there quietly, Kali, where the light makes it easy to see into your throat. Open your mouth wide, and relax

all you can. Turn your head a little. That's it. The mirror shows the bone clearly now. Forceps, please, Daudi. Kali, try not to swallow. It will not hurt much.'

The boy's eyes showed that he understood. The forceps grasped the bone; a deft movement, and it was out.

Afterwards Kali wanted to look at the instrument which had brought his trouble into view. It was a special surgical mirror, shaped like a tiny saucer. He held it close to his face and saw the tip of his nose and blinked. That mirror made his skin look like Hippo's.

'Kah, this mirror doesn't tell the truth, Bwana Daudi. It makes things look bigger than they are.'

'True, but this is very useful to find bones and things when they are stuck in your throat. Would you like to hear a story that helps you to understand about the mirror that always shows you exactly what you look like?'

'Always?' asked Kali.

'Exactly?' asked Tali.

Daudi nodded.

'Tell us about it now, Bwana Daudi.'

The Medical Assistant smiled, 'Now is the time of work. Sunset is the time for stories.'

And at sunset Daudi watched Tali and Kali lift Gulu out of the barrow and sit him on a three-legged stool.

'Is Hippo's foot bigger than this stool?' asked Gulu.

'Two or three times larger,' said Daudi.

Now, one day Dic-Dic and Toto watched Boohoo, the hippo, place his very large foot into a pool beside the river and peer down into it hopefully. His reflection disappeared in rippling water and little eddies of mud.

'This always happens,' he complained, 'and I would very much like to see EX-ACTLY what I look like.'

Toto, the monkey, who was having great difficulty trying to crack a coconut, watched him and heard him mumble, 'It would – *um* – be awful to look like poor Aunt Soso or even Cousin Boko; it's – *er* – very com-forting to be – *um* – what is that word … '

His sigh changed into a yawn and Dic-Dic shuddered as he saw a set of huge uneven teeth and a mouth that looked like a huge cave. He thought how ugly Hippo's nose looked, especially the bristles that stuck out of it.

Suddenly an idea came to life in Toto's monkey mind. He beckoned to Dic-Dic and together they ran down to the water's edge. Toto said politely, 'Boohoo, you have wonderful teeth.'

Boohoo blinked, '*Er* – what was that you said, little Monkey? Oh, yes, teeth. Very useful, and – *er* –'

'Handsome,' said Toto quickly. 'If I could show you how handsome you are, would you crack my coconut for me with your very fine teeth?'

Hippo came splashing out of the pool. '*Er* – handsome. Yes. That's the word I wanted.' Some of the droop disappeared from the corners of his mouth. 'It makes a great – *er* – difference to be hand-some, you know, Toto. You feel different.'

Toto nodded. 'Yes. And you have wonderful sturdy legs. *Er* – would you like to crack my coconut now?' He shuffled his feet impatiently.

Boohoo blinked at his stubby, mud-covered legs.

There was pride in his voice as he said, 'I can swim like a fish.' He lifted up one leg after the other and looked at it carefully before saying, '*Er* – one of the things I like about my legs is that I can see them. It would be nice to – *er* – but I was for-getting. You're going to show me ex-actly what I look like, aren't you, Toto? Will I see my – *er* – eyes and my – *um* – ears?'

'Yes! Yes!' said Toto, jumping up and down, 'but what about cracking my coconut?'

'*Er* – coconut? Ohhh, that! You want me to crack it, do you? I can eas-ily. Put it between my teeth.'

Toto did so and skipped aside hurriedly as the huge mouth slammed shut. 'Open again!' he urged. 'Boohoo, please open again!'

Hippo swallowed slowly and then said, '*Er* – you mean open my mouth, little Monkey?'

'Please!' cried Toto, 'and don't swallow my coconut!'

As the great mouth opened Boohoo's voice came from deep inside, 'You don't want me to swa-llow it, *eh?*'

Nimbly Toto collected all the bits of coconut that hadn't already disappeared. He backed away as Boohoo said, 'Now take me to – *er* – see myself.'

Toto pointed to a tumbledown palm-leaf house. 'Go in there,' he said, 'and keep your eyes wide open.'

'This will be a dreadful shock for poor old Boohoo,' muttered Dic-Dic. He turned, 'Boohoo, don't … '

But Boohoo wasn't listening. He was quivering with excitement. Dic-Dic had to jump hastily out of the way of a huge foot as Hippo lumbered towards the house.

'Ex-actly what I look like,' he said gently to himself. 'Wouldn't this be an awful ex-per-ience for Aunt Soso or Cousin Boko!'

He walked through the hole where the door had been and saw nothing special, so he squeezed his way into another room and saw to his amazement another hippo. Boohoo shut his eyes tight and thought, 'Oh dear, what a shame to be as ugly as – *er* – that one.'

He moved a little and the other hippo disappeared.

'Funny,' mumbled Boohoo, 'I'm sure there was another hippo here.' He turned slowly around and called to small Monkey, 'Did you – *er* – by any chance see another hip-po-pot-a-mus here?'

Toto scampered up to the top of a palm-tree, gulped down a mouthful of coconut, shaded his eyes, and looked around.

'There's no one here but us, Boohoo,' he shouted.

'*Er* – nobody? Really? Are you sure? What about you, Dic-Dic, did you – *um* – see – *er* … ?'

Dic-Dic shook his head. He didn't know what to say.

'Odd,' muttered Boohoo, 'most un-usual.'

Slowly, carefully, he made his way back into the room. There was the hippo again. He looked closely. Those looked very much like his feet and knees. An uncomfortable thought started to grow in his mind. He saw two hippo eyes open wide in alarm. Below them was a pimply, bristly, not at all good-looking nose.

Boohoo opened his mouth. The mouth in front of him opened too. He saw a set of huge teeth and shut his mouth tight in disgust. The other mouth slammed shut also.

The thought in his mind was growing clearer. He felt two big hippo tears running down his cheeks. Two big tears ran down the face that looked back at him.

Dic-Dic, who was standing a little behind, said softly, 'Remember, you swim very well indeed, Boohoo.'

But Boohoo wasn't listening. He was looking very closely at his reflection. Slow hot anger crept through his hippo mind.

'No! I don't believe it. I don't believe it all!' He lifted one great foot and pushed it hard against the mirror. There was a strange sharp sound, and a tinkling noise, then silence.

Boohoo peered in front of him. Nothing looked back at him now. 'That's better,' he sighed. 'Oh – *um* – good. It's gone now.' He shook his head slowly and walked thoughtfully back to the river. 'Ex-actly what I look like. What a silly – *um* – idea. *Er* – what a very – *um* – stupid idea!'

The water was cool and comforting. The water lily roots on the far bank were juicy. He lay in the mud with only his nostrils above the water. Through his mind again and again went the thought, 'I don't very much care for mirrors.'

Daudi stopped and looked at the eager faces around him. Yuditi shook her head. 'Hippo had small wisdom.'

Gogo drew pictures in the dust with his toe. 'It wasn't the mirror that did not tell the truth.'

'True,' nodded Daudi. 'It was the thoughts inside Hippo's head which were wrong. Ordinary mirrors show you your face as it is, not what you hope it looks like. But the great Mirror that God has given

us – the Bible – look in that and you will see exactly what God sees when he looks at your soul: nothing covered up, nothing made to look better than it is. In it you find God's way to change your whole life. You find the answer to your doubts and worries. You find the path that God has drawn up especially for you to follow to do the special job that he has planned for you. The thing of great importance is that you USE this Mirror and do not follow the wisdom of hippos.

'Listen! These are the words of God's Book itself – "The man who simply hears the message and does nothing about it is like a man catching the reflection of his own face in a mirror. But the man who looks into the perfect mirror of God's law, the law of liberty, and makes a habit of so doing, is not the man who sees and forgets. He puts the law into practice and he wins true happiness".'

Daudi paused, 'What is the best habit you can make?'

'To read God's Book frequently?' asked Gogo.

'Right,' nodded Daudi, 'to look into the great Mirror at least as often as you use an ordinary one.'

* * *

What's Inside the Fable?

Special Message: The Bible will show you how you should live.

Read *Matthew 4:4*

Read *Hebrews 4:12*

3

BUT HIPPOS ARE DIFFERENT

Kali and Tali hurried to Gogo's house. They found Goha, Dan, Elizabeti and Yuditi were already there roasting peanuts.

'Hongo,' said Kali, 'there is trouble in our family. My uncle, Mukamu has a mind that is hard to change. He talks in a loud voice and refuses to have vaccination.'

'Hongo,' went on Tali, 'he says the trouble is caused by the evil spirits.'

'Let's go and talk to him,' said Goha.

'It will be a matter of small usefulness, for behold, his eyes are shut to the new ways.'

'We must warn him,' said Goha.

'He will have fierce words,' sighed Tali.

However, they went one behind the other along a path that led into a group of baobab trees. Goha stood forward and greeted Mukamu, who sat in the shade.

'Great One, we have come to tell you of the disease called smallpox. It is a trouble that ...'

'Nyamale! Shut up!' roared Mukamu.

'But, Great One,' smiled Elizabeti, 'the way to stop it is simple. Also it produces little trouble; it is merely a scratching of the skin and ...'

'Kah!' Mukamu spat, 'Nyamale nye, shut up all of you!'

'You perhaps are right, Great One,' said Yuditi, 'my arm swelled a little a week after the Bwana scratched it, but ...'

'I'm not going to have any of this medicine,' growled Mukamu.

'Yoh!' said Tali, 'and I was unable to eat for two days after, but ...'

Mukamu startled them with his loud laughter.

Elizabeti stood in front of the others and held her arm out for inspection. 'See, it is but a small scar, less than the size of your thumb-nail, but because of it I am secure from this sickness.'

'Why?' sneered Mukamu, 'Why? You don't know why!'

'It's all in the Bwana Doctor's big book.'

'Kah! How do you know the book is right? Clear out! Take your noise to other places. I will not do this thing!'

'We have warned you, Great One,' said Kali.

BUT HIPPOS ARE DIFFERENT

Mukamu picked up his knobbed stick. The children ran.

Daudi heard the story that evening. 'You did right. This matter of warnings is very important. You know, once Boohoo, the hippo, heard the warning voice of Elephant, but he didn't think that it was meant for him ...'

'What happened, Bwana Daudi?'

They settled down among the roots of the buyu tree.

'Hongo,' said Daudi, 'Once ...

Near the great mountains that hide their heads in the clouds there was considerable lightning and much thunder and tremendous rain. Soon a great flood came raging down upon the jungle. Elephant trumpeted loud and long. The sound of his warning reached to every ear in the whole jungle. Some that heard the news of danger hurried to high ground where there was safety for their hides, scales or feathers.

But there were also many who, although their ears heard, and although their minds understood, they did nothing about it.

Among them was a hyena who lay deep in a hole that he had dug in the soft, cool earth not far from the river bank. Here he had piles of bones which promised joy to his stomach. 'Does he think I'd leave these?' he snarled, and closed his ears to the voice of Elephant, and to the crash of thunder.

There was a jackal who turned his back on the dark clouds and looked towards the shining moon. 'Who'd take any notice of Elephant?' he sneered.

He made his way under a great flat rock, and curled up. 'No rain will come in here. Who's scared of thunderstorms? I've seen hundreds of them. There's never been a time when the river came up here.'

He heard the Elephant's trumpeting, more urgently this time, but he shrugged his jackal shoulders, laid his ears flat against his head and went to sleep.

Hippo heard and thought, 'Oh dear! Thunderstorms, the – *um* – river will be muddy, and that always irr-itates my nose. I like clear water to swim in. *Er* – what was that Elephant was saying? Oh – *um* – danger. Come up on to the – *er* – high ground where it is safe ... '

A worried look moved around Hippo's large face. 'I hope the others will take notice. It's very important for them. But I'm diff-er-ent of course. I can swim like a fish. Sometimes I like being in water more than I like being

on the land. It's less – *um* – work to swim than to – *um* – walk. Oh, I do hope they'll take – *um* – notice of Elephant.'

And to show what a very good swimmer he was, he dived to the bottom of the river and thought how interesting the lightning looked through water lily leaves.

He thought, 'I only hope Rhino takes notice of what he's heard. He's so very ob-stin-ate, is Rhino. And bad tempered too. So unlike me. I'm … '

Behind him he felt as though some great creature was pushing. 'Stop that!' muttered Boohoo. 'Don't – *er* – You're – *um* – .'

He found himself hurled to one side and rolling over and over. He swam with his great strong legs, but it didn't help him.

BANG! An awful pain went down his back legs. He was tossed about like a twig in that vast torrent.

WALLOP! Most of the wind was driven out of his lungs by something that felt like the kick of six elephants. His hippo mind suddenly understood that the warning had been for him too.

He was under water. The air in his lungs was nearly exhausted. Everywhere around him, and above him was rushing, swirling water. He was

whirled to the surface. He took a gulping breath. It was half water and half air. He coughed and sneezed, and THUMP!

His hippo mind stopped working.

From where he stood, high above the flood on the mountainside, Dic-Dic saw Hippo tossed about in the current. He came up swimming and struggling only to crash head first into a pile of boulders. The current swung him on to a mudbank. He lay there terribly still, his head resting against an egg-shaped rock. With horror Dic-Dic saw the large round nostrils slip slowly down into the water.

He rushed downhill, leaped over some big pools and dashed to Hippo's side just as the great nose sank beneath the surface.

Frantically Dic-Dic tried to splash the water out of the pool beside the rock so that Hippo could breathe, but it was no use, more water kept running in.

Taking a deep breath, Dic-Dic forced his body under the great head and heaved. Nothing happened.

He wriggled till his strong little legs were firmly on the bottom, and tried again. He felt the great head lift a little. He heaved again and saw the hippo nostrils come to the surface with water trickling out of them. But Dic-Dic knew he couldn't hold on for long. His knees ached, his muscles trembled, his spine started to bend.

Suddenly there was the sound of galloping hooves then a loud splash. Vaguely around him he saw Twiga's legs then the long powerful neck took the weight from his shoulders.

'Try and prop his head up with something,' panted Twiga.

Dic-Dic staggered towards a pile of driftwood, found a big piece and put it in place under Hippo's chin.

'Poor Boohoo,' gasped Twiga, 'he's badly knocked about. Those who ignore warnings find themselves in terrible trouble. Everyone heard Elephant's trumpeting, "To safety! To safety!" And those who obeyed are safe now.'

'But,' said Dic-Dic, 'the others who didn't, what happened to them?'

Twiga shook his head sadly, 'I have seen many creatures tossed downstream by the anger of this torrent. They all had reasons of their own for taking no notice of the warning, and they all thought they were very good reasons indeed.'

Boohoo slowly opened one eye and groaned.

'Oh!' said Twiga, 'see! He's all right!'

Boohoo made a tremendous effort, but his voice was not doing what he told it. At last, from his swollen, bruised lips, came, 'Did you say, ALL RIGHT? Oh dear, I was sure that what Elephant was telling the jungle didn't really mean me. Oh dear ...'

On three legs he struggled over to a great pool of mud in the shade and sank down into it. Many of the other members of the jungle passing that way stopped and looked at Boohoo. His only reply to their questions was, '*Um* – oh dear ...!'

'Do you think,' said Dic-Dic, 'that Boohoo will do what Elephant says next time?'

Twiga put his head on one side. 'Who knows? But it is certain that all who listen to what Elephant says and do what he advises, are not caught in floods, anywhere, any time.'

The children nodded, and saying a soft 'Goodbye' disappeared into the dusk.

A week later the twins came to visit Daudi. 'Great One, who should have been attacked by this smallpox trouble but our Uncle Mukamu.' They shook their heads. 'His sickness is very great.'

'Hongo, if only he'd listened to the warning,' said Tali as they walked towards the buyu tree.

'But,' said Gulu, 'Boohoo took no notice of the warnings and nothing much happened to him.'

'Hongo,' said Daudi, 'being nearly drowned, having many broken ribs and a thousand bruises, of course, are nothing!'

Goha laughed. 'THAT warning was underlined with aches. But if he kept on taking no notice, what then?'

'He would not escape,' said Daudi. 'Remember, God is very kind and patient, but if we take no notice of what he tells us to do or not to do, it is our fault entirely when trouble comes.'

'What does the Bible say about warnings?' asked Gogo.

'Many, many things. There are gentle, kind words; there are short, sharp ones that say "Don't", or "Stop". There are strong, fearless stories that tell of men who took warnings and what happened to them, and others who did not and the great trouble they found. The words of the great Mirror are summed up in this question:

HOW SHALL WE ESCAPE IF WE NEGLECT SUCH A GREAT A SALVATION?

'Does neglect mean turn your back on?' asked Elizabeti.

'Exactly that,' said Daudi. 'Also it means TAKE NO NOTICE OF.'

* * *

What's Inside the Fable?

Special Message: Listen to what God says in the Bible and obey.

Read *Hebrews 2:3*

4
THE WISDOM OF DONKEYS

'Kah,' said Tali, 'we don't know what to do, Bwana Daudi. Many of those we tell about the usefulness of being made safe from smallpox say, "Maybe we'll come for help".'

'Ngheeh,' agreed Kali, 'and others say, "Perhaps we'll go to the hospital tomorrow." Their minds wander and they chose no path.'

'Eheh,' said Daudi, 'their ways are well known. We will talk of this matter at sunset.'

That evening Gulu and Liso travelled from the hospital to the buyu tree on the back of an old and very good-natured donkey. As Daudi lifted the children off his back, the donkey raised his head high in the air and brayed.

'Yoh!' laughed Goha, 'does he not make noises very much like those of zebra?'

'Eheh,' said Daudi. 'They are very close relations.

43

Have you not heard the story of how zebra came to have stripes? This is a story that comes from far inside the country of dreams.'

Punda, the small donkey, was full of sadness. Within his skin there was nothing but unhappiness. He looked with envy at the animals under the *buyu* tree. 'Hee-haw!' he brayed sadly, 'You are lucky, Twiga. Your skin is golden and mottled like the sunlight and shadow under thorntrees, but mine is just black. Look at Lion, his colour is tawny like the tall grasses. And little Dic-Dic here, he is brown and comfortable-looking. But I, Punda, am black, just black.'

He sighed from deep down within him and ground his big square teeth in a way that made Hippo shiver as he lay in the river with only the top of his head showing.

'*Er* – I wish you wouldn't do that with your teeth, Punda. It makes my skin creep, you know. And – *um* – what's wrong with a black skin, any-way? Use-ful, I – *er* – think. Doesn't show the dirt.'

Boohoo made a noise so like laughter that Dic-Dic nearly fell over with surprise. But Punda stood with his head down, his ears down, his tail drooping, the very picture of misery, unhappiness and dejection.

'Hee-haw!' he brayed, rolling his eyes, 'do you wonder I want to be shiny and white? Oh how I wish … '

Boohoo blew bubbles slowly through his large and bristly nose. '*Um*,' he remarked, '*Er* – one of my aunts told me when I was very small that there is an – *um* – sort of cave place under the – *er* – moun-tains that rumble near the swamp, that helps in this kind of thing ... ' Boohoo stopped for breath. '*Er* – she said it trans – *er* – trans-forms – *er* – it changes your colour.'

Punda pricked up his ears. 'Helps you to change colour?'

Hippo absentmindedly munched water-lily leaves.

Donkey ground his teeth. 'Tell me or I'll kick you!'

Hippo shook his head, '*Er* –don't do that. My aunt bit a donkey once. It was awful. They say that ... '

Punda stamped his feet. 'What about this cave?'

'Oh, yes, the dark one in the moun-tains that rumble you mean? Oh – *er* – she said – but mind you, I don't know if it's true or not ...'

Donkey pranced on his hind legs, but Boohoo just went on. 'She said – *er* – if you go through the hole near the water-fall, and go right inside till the light is only as big as a fire-fly, and then call loudly, but –

45

er – Punda, it's a large and creepy and echo-ey cave. If I were – *er* – if I were you – *um* – I'd ...'

'What did she say? Hurry up, Boohoo! What do you do in the cave?'

'Oh, yes, the cave. Oh, you only have to – *um* – wish ...'

'Wish? How?'

Boohoo's forehead wrinkled with concentration. '*Er* – yes, you could wish that your colour would – *er* ...'

But Punda was off at a gallop, his mind full of the idea of being white.

He passed the great swamp, and took no notice of Crocodile. He went up the long slope that led to the dark mountain, and hardly looked at Hyena and Vulture. He paused at the bottom of the cliff where he saw a hole that led into the heart of the mountain.

He put his head in and hee-hawed. A frightening lot of hee-haws came back at him, and something black clutched at his face. Punda stumbled back but found to his relief that it was only Budi, the bat.

Donkey felt an empty feeling inside him, and his hair all stuck up and felt prickly. He stumbled on and on in the dark until he could only just see the place where he had come in. He took a deep breath, swallowed hard, and rather squeakily his voice came, 'Please, I want to be white.'

'... BE WHITE...BE WHITE ... be white ...' went the echo.

Just to be sure, he called again, and again the echo came back.

'... WHITE ... WHITE ... white ...'

He stumbled towards the tiny patch of light, and as he came closer his heart beat faster. Would it have happened? Would he be white?

The patch grew larger and larger. He forced his body through the gap in the rock and staggered out. The sunlight dazzled him and he sneezed. Then he looked down at his feet. He looked at his left legs. He looked at his right legs. They were white. He turned round and swished his tail. It was white. And then to his delight he realised he WAS white, every bit of him.

He hee-hawed with joy, kicked up his heels and cantered back towards the jungle, his mind full of happiness. He was white and shining, and, he thought, BEAUTIFUL. He trotted down to the river and looked at himself in a clear pool.

'Oh,' said Hippo, 'you went to the – *er* – place I told you about.'

'Yes,' smiled Punda.

From above Vulture squawked, 'Look at that! A white donkey! What a joke!'

A small doubt passed through Punda's mind. He looked into the pool again and what he saw mirrored there relieved his mind greatly until he heard Crocodile's loud voice, 'You stupid donkey, black is better for you!'

Punda kept looking into the water and tried to take no notice. Then Hyena came shambling out of the shadows. He filled the jungle with horrid laughter. 'How silly can you get, eh?'

'Rubbish!' said Dic-Dic, 'you look splendid.'

Boohoo came lumbering out of the water. 'I – er – think it looks very nice, too. Er ... ' One huge foot landed in a puddle, SPLASH! – and white donkey was spotted all over with mud. Hippo stopped and peered at him. 'Er – that is to say, I'm not sure that it suits you. It shows the dirt somewhat.'

Punda was dazed. He stood gazing into the distance. He wanted to go to a quiet place and think things over. He splashed out of the pool and walked slowly up a winding path. Hyena's jeering voice followed him. 'Can't even keep your feet clean now!'

Small Donkey looked down and saw the mud sticking to all his four legs. He stopped in the shade of the *buyu* tree and shook his head. 'Probably it was better the old way,' he muttered.

Boohoo came over to him and said confidentially, '*Er* – why not brush it off, Punda? That – *er* – might help.'

Again Punda had a comforting feeling of relief. With excitement in his hooves he galloped off and rolled over and over in the sand. This helped quite a lot but the dark spots were still there.

Boohoo was looking at him with his head on one side, '*Er* – why not try the – *er* – river?' he mumbled. 'I always – *er* – find that – *er* ... '

But Punda was already on his way to the water. He plunged in and swam and swam and swam. Back on the river bank he shook himself hopefully.

Vulture flapped his wings in his face and screeched, 'Spotty, the donkey! Spotty, the donkey!'

Jackal jibed, 'Spots and blots, spots and blots!'

Hyena's sarcastic voice filled that corner of the jungle, 'You never noticed the dirt before, did you, Spotty?'

Dic-Dic came up to him and said, 'Cheer up, Punda. There are ways of getting rid of every single spot.'

But little Donkey's thinking was so muddled that he didn't take any notice.

Dic-Dic pranced around him and said cheerfully, 'I like it. It suits you.'

But Punda sighed again and plodded off towards the echoey cave in the dark mountain, muttering, 'I should have known it wouldn't work. I should never have gone near that cave at all.'

Dic-Dic walked silently beside him for a long, long way. Once Punda stopped and fixed his large sad eyes on little Antelope. 'I wish I knew what to do!'

'Come back with me now,' urged Dic-Dic. 'You look much better like this.'

Punda hesitated. Ahead was the mist over the mountain. From behind came the laughter of hyenas. He glanced unhappily at his much stained legs, and moved slowly on.

Dic-Dic tried very hard to make Punda see how really good the change was. But his only answer was the weary clop, clop, clop of Punda's hooves.

When they came to the cave he tried to stop Punda going in, but Donkey nosed him slowly aside and pushed his way into the dark opening.

The gloom of the cave frightened him. Suddenly he thought, 'There is quite a lot to be said for light and for being white.' But he stumbled on. It was black and ominous all around. 'Black!' he whispered. It echoed weirdly, B L A C K ... BLACK ... Black.'

Something seemed to get into him. He reared up and brayed loudly, 'I want to be black!'

'BLACK ... BLACK ... Black!' shouted the echo.

But even as he heard it he knew he liked being white better. He shuffled towards the cave entrance. Outside he blinked in the glare, then he saw his right legs. They were black. He looked at his left legs. They were black. He whisked his tail. It was black too.

Dic-Dic stared in amazement.

Over the western hills the sun was setting. Punda sat down on his tail and hee-hawed in misery, for he didn't really know what he wanted.

Day followed day. The jungle was full of talk about Punda. One liked him this way. One liked him that. He moved around from one to the other. 'You are better black,' said one. 'I like you white,' said another. He turned to this one and that and the more he turned the dizzier he became; and the dizzier he became the less he knew what he wanted to be.

In despair one day he galloped off through the jungle not knowing what to do, and he found himself once more at the entrance of the cave. He pushed his way in hardly noticing the rumbling noises and the clouds of dust that swirled around him. He stopped and at the top of his donkey voice he brayed, 'I want to be black, and I want to be white, I want to be ... and the echo came back,

'BLACK and WHITE ... BLACK and WHITE ... Black and White ...'

Suddenly the echo was lost in a deep ominous rumble. A great stone fell at Punda's feet and another hit him on the back. He turned and bolted towards the opening where the light still came through dimly.

As he pushed his shoulders through the opening he felt the walls trembling and stones and earth came tumbling down. He galloped out on to the plain as, with a tremendous rumbling, huge rocks fell and the doorway closed for ever.

At long last Punda stopped galloping and a great lump came into his throat as he looked down at his left leg, and then at his right. He rolled his eyes in dismay. 'Oh no, it cannot be! It just cannot be!' he gasped as he realized he was striped from nose to hoof to tail tip. 'I'm black *and* white!'

Elizabeti clapped her hands, 'He became zebra because he couldn't make up his mind!'

'That's it,' nodded Daudi, 'but see the warning. A time came when his mind was made up for him. He had no more chances.

'When your eyes see zebras or stripes, let your mind remember two things, two pictures you will see in the great Mirror: first, of those who make the greatest mistake of all by not making up their minds to become Christians; and then of those who try to serve both God and the devil. The Bible says this can't be done, and calls it DOUBLE-MINDEDNESS.

'Jesus wants us to be members of His family and to be single-hearted not double-minded.'

* * *

What's Inside the Fable?

Special Message: Don't put off making a decision to follow the Lord.

Read *James 1:8 and James 4:8*

5

THE TEAM GAME

'At weddings,' said Elizabeti, 'the girls show their joy by making trills with their tongues.'

'Like this,' broke in Liso. She made a loud and cheerful noise. 'To do it you make your tongue move from side to side very fast.'

Jungle Doctor laughed. 'My tongue is only used to moving backwards and forwards.'

'You become good at trilling with practise,' smiled the African girl.

As she spoke, people came hurrying past the hospital singing and drumming and whistling and trilling.

'I wouldn't miss this wedding for anything,' laughed Yuditi as she and Elizabeti each took one of Liso's arms and hurried off towards the church.

'Bwana,' said Goha, 'the two who are to be married were amongst the very first to be vaccinated. They both think the same way about things.'

At sunset the drums were still going in the village. The children had come back to the buyu tree. Elizabeti was excited. 'It was a wedding of joy today.'

Yuditi nodded her head.

Daudi turned to them. 'Were you girls thinking of the day when you would be married?'

Elizabeti covered her face with her hands and Yuditi giggled.

'Bwana Daudi, how did you know that we often think of these matters?'

Daudi smiled. 'You do right. It is a thing of wisdom to see what the great Mirror has to tell you about the person that God has for you to share your life with.'

'Hongo,' said Yuditi, 'does the Bible help us in this matter also?'

'Of course,' nodded Daudi. 'It is a book that God has prepared for all who become members of his family. He wants to show us the best way to live.'

'Well, what should we do?' asked Kali.

'Let Bwana Daudi tell his story,' whispered Gogo. 'The answer will be there for those with open ears.'

Daudi leaned forward on the three-legged stool.

Dic-Dic looked up at Hippo. 'They say that at the time of the ripening of watermelons there is a special jungle sport.'

'*Er – um* – yes,' said Boohoo sadly. '*Er* – watermelons, did you say? I like watermelons.' His mouth started watering so uncomfortably that he lumbered off to the lake and swam gently along thinking such delightful thoughts of watermelons that he did not hear Elephant calling all the animals together.

Elephant told them carefully all about it. Eyes grew round as he showed them the prize. His final words were, 'Think about it carefully, and return here after two sunrises; and if anyone wants me to tell them the best way to do it, I'll … '

'Simple,' shouted Rhino. 'All I have to do to win that watermelon is to pull that large flat stone in a straight line along the broad place of white sand.'

'Not exactly,' said Tembo. 'It's TWO who do the pulling, not just one.'

Rhino snorted. 'That means I'll have to share. Pity. I'd better find Hippo. He's about the same size, and we both like watermelons. I'll bring him back on Sports Day.'

Toto watched Rhino gallop off in a cloud of dust. 'He won't even taste one watermelon seed. Dic-Dic, you and I will play it together. We'll win it easily.'

'Mm,' said Dic-Dic, 'won't it be difficult if you walk on your back legs and I go on all four feet at once?'

'No trouble,' chuckled Monkey, 'I'm adaptable, and anyhow we both want that watermelon, don't we?'

Dic-Dic nodded. Thoughtfully he trotted off to have a look at the long 'Y' shaped vine that had loops on two ends of it for the necks of those who pulled, and the big flat stone tied to the third end.

Toto started turning somersaults in the sand and then he picked up the large flat stone to show how strong he was.

Dic-Dic bounded on to an anthill and called, 'Toto, don't you think we ought to talk to Elephant? He's very wise, and ... '

'You can if you like,' panted Toto, who had noticed that Goon and Loon the baboons were watching him. He puffed out his chest and lifted the stone above his head.

Twiga and the graceful young giraffe who nibbled the shoots of the umbrella tree with him, went and talked for a long time with Elephant, who finished by pointing with his trunk to a strange shaped tree on the side of a hill.

As they walked away together Twiga said, 'There's only one way to have real success in this team game. What Elephant says is right.' They stood looking at the tree in the distance.

Two days later all the animals came to the long stretch of white sand. Rhino's loud voice made everybody look up. 'Come on, will you, Hippo! We both have four feet and two eyes and stomachs that welcome watermelons, haven't we? What more do you want, eh?'

Boohoo hung back. '*Er* – I'd rather play this game with another hippo. *Um* – hippos understand other hippos best, you know.'

'What rot!' roared Rhino. 'We're about the same height, and the same weight. We're near enough. Come on, let's get cracking.'

Boohoo's voice was slow and reluctant. 'Oh – er – very well. But I'd much rather sit in the shade just now. My skin sun-burns very eas-ily, you know. Most uncomfort-able. But you wouldn't under-stand – er ...'

'Come on! COME ON! COME ON!' grated Rhino. 'We'll be all right. Anyway, don't you want any water-melon?'

'Er – no, that is to say, yes, but if you were a hippo you'd know this sand is very hot. It's very irr-irritat – er – it always makes me itchy.'

He trudged along unhappily towards the starting place muttering that he'd catch a terrible cold in this awful heat. Suddenly he stopped and tried to press his upper-lip with his front foot. Rhino glared at him. 'Come on, stick-in-the-mud, COME ON!'

'Oh dear,' gulped Hippo, 'I'b going to, I'b going to sneeze. Hip-hip-hipposhoo ... ! Oh dear, now my – um – eyes will start to run, my nose will start to run ...'

'Yes,' said Rhino, 'and if your – um – feet don't start to run soon, I'll do something about it.'

He jerked the loop of vine over his horn and around his neck. 'Let's go.'

Hippo nosed his way into his end of the long vine. '*Er* – where are we going? Wouldn't it be – *um* – better if we had a look before we start-ed?'

'Stop talking! Stop grumbling! Let's go. Action, that's what we want.' Rhino stamped his feet impatiently. A cloud of dust rose.

'*Er* – dust always makes me want to – *um* – sneeze,' said Hippo. 'Very – *um* – in-con-sid-er-ate of you it is.'

From the top of the umbrella-tree Twiga shook his head gently. 'What a team! What a track they will make! How can two different animals succeed even if they are almost the same size?'

Stripey, the zebra, called, 'Both ready?'

'Of course we're ready,' roared Rhino.

'The straightest path wins,' shouted Stripey. 'Go!'

Eight large feet drove deep into the sand.

Rhino peered short-sightedly past his horn. His breathing sounded like a cross-cut saw. Hippo kept up with him as well as he could, the stone bouncing along behind leaving a bumpy track in the sand.

'Faster!' ground out Rhino.

'*Er* – but ...' panted Hippo. He blinked his eyes as he saw in front of him a tall palm-tree. '*Er* – shouldn't we – *er* – a-void – *er* – that – *er* ...'

'Give your chin a rest and get on with it!'

Faru's head was down, his eyes were half closed. Hippo saw the palm-tree loom up in front. He pulled to one side to dodge it.

'What do you think you're doing?' panted Rhino. 'How do you expect to win anything if you ... ?'

'But you see ... in front is ... '

'*Pish!*' interrupted Rhino. 'Run straight, will you ...'

BING! He caught the tree with his great shoulder and staggered. A shower of coconuts came down.

BONG! One crashed down on Rhino's nose.

BONG! Another landed between Boohoo's eyes.

Rhino's eyes went red, dangerously red. 'What do you think you're doing, you clumsy skinful of misery?' He dashed forward jerking the great stone, which shot through the air and landed WHAM! just above where his tail started.

With a roar of rage Faru shook his head clear of the loop of vine, kicked Hippo in the ribs and dashed off wildly into the denser parts of the jungle.

Boohoo sat down hard with all the wind knocked out of him. When at last his eyes would focus properly he saw the twisty broken path that the great stone had made. '*Er* – we didn't do very well, did we? *Er* – we were some-what a-like, but not – *um* – very. It's a pity we hadn't – *er* – thought about it more be-fore we started.'

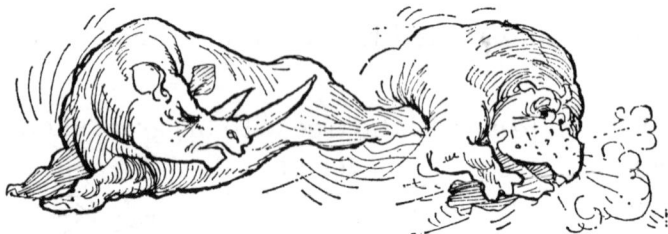

Daudi stopped telling the story and looked up the path towards a nurse who was hurrying towards them.

'*Bwana Daudi, come quickly!*' *she called.*

'*Coming,*' *answered Daudi, and over his shoulder as he ran, 'stay here. I'll finish this story tonight.*'

The sun set and it became quite dark. The crickets started chirping and a hyena howled way behind the hospital.

'*Hongo,*' *said Yuditi, 'what is behind this story?*'

'*He's saying that people who marry should think very carefully before they do so,*' *said Gogo.*

Dan nodded. 'Did he not say that today's wedding was one of joy for both Kefa and Marita are Christians?'

'Ngheeh,' agreed Elizabeti, 'did we not hear them say they both wanted to live the same way with God in charge of their lives?'

Liso slapped at a mosquito and said, 'Does he mean that those who are Christians shouldn't marry those who aren't?'

They discussed things in low voices. The sound of hyena was coming closer.

Elizabeti whispered, 'I wish Bwana Daudi would hurry.'

'It's all right,' said Goha, 'Kali and I both have knobbed sticks. Um, there he is now.'

Daudi came hurrying out of the ward, only to disappear into another lighted doorway.

'Bwana Doctor, lend me a lamp, please. I've not finished my story to the children yet.'

'What's it about tonight, Daudi?'

'Life partners; that now is the time to start praying about this, and I'm telling them what the Bible says.'

'This is a thing of high importance, Daudi. Many people wreck their lives by not knowing or not obeying God in this matter.'

Daudi hurried to the buyu tree. His lamp showed the children sitting close together in the darkness. 'What's happened so far?'

'Rhino and Hippo made an awful mess,' said Gogo.

'And now, what do you think happened to Toto, the monkey, and Dic-Dic, the antelope?'

'Tell us! Tell us! Tell us!' cried the girls.

Daudi nodded.

Toto said to Dic-Dic, 'Come on. Rhino and Hippo won't be hard to beat.'

Small Antelope nodded. 'They hadn't much idea of the way they were going. Now listen, Toto, you and I understand each other. We'll both go together on four legs instead of two.'

As Toto slipped the loop over his head he saw Goon and Loon, the baboons, whispering with Hyena and Jackal. 'Watch me, fellers!' he yelled, sticking out his chest and bunching up his muscles.

Dic-Dic pushed him gently with his chin. 'We must both keep our thoughts on making that stone move straight if we are going to win the watermelon.'

'*Um* – yes, watermelon,' said Toto, thinking how important he looked.

Dic-Dic whispered to himself, 'Everything will be all right when we're actually going and pulling together.' To help himself to believe this he whispered still louder, 'I'm sure it will be all right. I know it will.'

'Go!' called Stripey.

Toto went down on all fours and away they went.

In the lower limbs of the *buyu* tree a score of small monkeys jumped up and down and shouted, 'Good old Toto!' For Toto and Dic-Dic were moving together stride for stride.

'How're you going, four legs?' shouted Goon.

Toto took no notice. It was hot work. 'Wouldn't a drink be good,' he thought, but he ran steadily on.

Under the *buyu* tree Jackal felt hot breath in his ear and heard Hyena's whisper. 'Keep your eyes on those trees, Slinki; they're full of monkey downfall.'

The sun blazed down. Antelope's shoulders started to ache. Toto licked his dry lips.

Chattering noisily Goon and Loon dashed through the treetops waving a bunch of bananas in the air. Toto could almost feel the cool smooth taste of bananas on his tongue.

Suddenly, high through the air towards him came a luscious ripe banana. It landed just beyond Toto's reach. He darted towards it. The stone jerked as, walking on his back feet, he gleefully grabbed it.

'Carefully,' panted Dic-Dic, 'we're going crooked.'

Another banana landed still farther from the track. Toto was after it in a flash. He scooped it up. The stone skidded sideways. Toto slipped the loop of the vine from round his shoulders and dashed off into the jungle clutching a banana in each hand.

Dic-Dic sat sadly in the sand and looked back at the track which went so straight for such a long way, and then twisted and ended up in an untidy pile of sand.

Jackal smirked. 'Easy! All we had to do with them was to talk of bananas to baboons.'

Hyena sneered. 'Easier still with Hippo and Rhino. We didn't need to do anything.' The sneer changed to a snarl, 'But we'll do no good at all with these two.' He looked over his shoulder to where Twiga was putting the loop of vine over the head of the graceful giraffe beside him, and heard him saying, 'It's our turn now. We both know the way. Two of the same kind. Two minds that think as one. Four eyes on the same spot. Legs that move together in the same direction.'

That is how they started, their eyes fixed on the tree in the distance. Over the hot sand moved the two giraffes, the strong muscles of their shoulders moving rhythmically as they shared the weight of the stone.

As they passed the finishing mark there was a long straight line in the sand behind

them. Boohoo nodded his head slowly, '*Er* – very power-ful are giraffes.'

'Yeah,' jeered Hyena, 'long skinny legs.'

'*Um,*' remarked Hippo, 'I once remember a hyena who – *er* – travelled a con-sider-able distance when – *um* – kicked by two of those long skinny legs.' He turned to Elephant, '*Er* – what was it you said, Tembo, about this team game?'

Daudi stopped. 'What is your answer to Boohoo's question?' Gogo answered, 'Two of the same species, each with the same wish in their heads and hearts.'

'Right,' said Daudi. 'The Bible says two things: "Do not be unequally yoked with unbelievers." That means in marriage or in any other partnership.'

'The yoke is the harness used for two animals in ploughing. They must pull together to produce a straight furrow. God says that for one of His family to marry or go into partnership with anyone who has not yet become a Christian is forbidden.' Daudi paused. 'If you live with your eyes open you will see the trouble that comes into the lives of those who disobey this command.'

Elizabeti said quietly, 'That is easy to understand. What other things does the Bible say?'

'Do two drummers bring food for the ears if their beat is not in rhythm?'

There was a shaking of heads.

Daudi went on. 'So it is that those who have become Christians need to travel in step. The Bible says, "How can two walk together unless they are agreed?" and the words of a wise man make the whole picture very clear: "Each for the other, and both for God".'

* * *

What's Inside the Fable?

Special Message: Keep in step with other Christians.

Read *2 Corinthians 6:14*

Read *Amos 3:3*

6

HOW TO TAKE THE WEIGHT OUT OF BURDENS

Everybody had arrived at the buyu tree except Gogo and Goha.

'Here they come!' cried Elizabeti.

Two figures came wearily up the hill.

'Hurry up!' called Kali and Tali.

'We can't hurry,' said Goha, 'we are too tired.'

They sank down on the ground at Daudi's feet, and Gogo said, 'Great One, our strength is finished. We've talked and talked to many people in many places today.'

Goha nodded. 'It is hard to make them understand.'

'It's worth it though,' chuckled Daudi, 'and maybe you've forgotten something. Listen to the great mistake that Dic-Dic made, and have a tongue loaded with answers when the story stops.'

One day in the jungle, Hifi, Toto's plump relation, made the mistake of finding three dead limbs in the one fall. When the first broke he swung on to another branch, and as that broke also his tail tightened around a thick old limb that looked strong, but unfortunately it had been part-eaten by white ants. Hifi hurtled down and landed safely but uncomfortably in a thorn bush. Only a second later the dead limb landed BANG! on his monkey head.

'*Er*,' said Hippo, 'it's just as well it was only his head. He might have broken his leg, you know.'

Hifi lay on the grass rolling his eyes. Dic-Dic said, 'I'll carry him back to his family tree.'

But it wasn't as easy as he thought, for Hifi was chubby and heavy, and he wriggled and kept calling for his Uncle Nyani and demanding a banana in a weak voice.

Dic-Dic's muscles started to ache as he battled along over the long jungle path. His steps grew slower and his legs began to wobble.

'*Er*,' said Hippo as he ambled along behind, 'he must be rather heavy. You're bending in the – *um* – middle, you know.'

Dic-Dic gasped. 'He is heavy. My neck's aching and my back's nearly breaking.' He staggered into the shade of what looked like a great grey boulder and put Hifi down. Monkey groaned and made loud noises of suffering and louder requests for food.

'He's rather heavy for a monkey,' said Boohoo.

Dic-Dic flopped down and panted, but said nothing.

'*Er*,' remarked Boohoo, 'would it be help-ful to drag him behind you on a banana leaf or something?'

Dic-Dic tried this, but Hifi yelled very loudly indeed.

Boohoo shook his head slowly and observed, '*Er* – no good. It seems to be un-com-fort-able for him.' He looked around carefully and said '*Um*' several times, but no ideas came into his mind, so he wrinkled up his forehead and tried to look important.

Dic-Dic sat there thinking how long was the road and how heavy was the monkey.

Hifi's groans became louder. The sun was very hot. Boohoo's head was nodding. Dic-Dic was in the middle of a sigh which abruptly turned into a gulp for the shade in which he sat started to move. Hifi nearly jumped out of his monkey skin when a long snake-like shadow moved towards them, but Dic-Dic knew at once that it was the trunk of Elephant, whose eyes twinkled at him, and whose deep voice said, 'Would you like to ride on my shoulders, Dic-Dic? They are very strong.'

Dic-Dic nodded gratefully. Hifi climbed on to Dic-Dic's back again and Elephant picked up small Antelope and the monkey burden and put them on his shoulder.

Soon Dic-Dic was making contented noises as they moved swiftly through the jungle. A cool breeze fanned his face.

Boohoo followed behind mumbling, '*Er* – very use-ful. I'd have done the same, Dic-Dic, you know, but hippos are at a great dis-ad-vant – ' he swallowed slowly, '*Er* – it is not so easy when you haven't got a trunk.'

As he lumbered along he noticed that Antelope's back was bending again in the same way as it had before. The beginnings of many thoughts started to wander about in his head. '*Er*,' he mumbled, '*Er* – Dic-Dic – *er* – are you … ?'

For a while Dic-Dic had felt the same old ache returning to his spine. He was struggling with all his strength to support Hifi, who was complaining in a very loud and irritating way.

All at once Dic-Dic realised that his back could not keep on carrying Hifi for much longer. The sound of Boohoo's voice made him turn a little. At once the weight of his monkey burden shifted and seemed to break in two. He started to slide. His feet tried to grip Elephant's neck, but they couldn't. He was slipping, slipping. 'Help!' he gasped. 'Help!' In a flash the long, strong trunk swung up and held him and his burden steady. 'Why are you still carrying Hifi?' came in a whisper from Elephant.

Dic-Dic couldn't think of an answer.

Boohoo's voice came vaguely from behind, '*Er* – look out, Dic-Dic, you nearly coll – that is, collap – *er* – you nearly fell off just then.'

Elephant said quietly, 'Dic-Dic, you are trusting me with your own weight, why not rest Hifi on my shoulders as well? There's plenty of room.'

'*Er* – yes,' came Hippo's voice, 'I was going to make that – *um* – sugg – *er* – sugg-es-tion, that's the word, isn't it? I was going to say, Why don't you, that is ...' He stopped as he saw Dic-Dic lean back gratefully against the strength of Elephant's trunk and say, 'But Tembo, it's so kind of you to carry me, how can I ask you to carry my load as well?'

Elephant chuckled. 'Think carefully, Dic-Dic. Think carefully.' The twinkle came into his eyes again as a very little while later he felt Hifi being gently placed on a spot just in front of Dic-Dic.

They moved on for a long way. The sun was still very hot. The path was still uphill, but Hifi was making the soft noises of monkey snoring, and Dic-Dic put his head on Elephant's trunk and rubbed very gently with his chin. He felt his happiness grow as a most comforting answering ripple came along the very strong muscles that supported him and his burden so carefully.

'*Um*,' came Hippo's voice, 'Why didn't you put Hifi on Elephant's back at the beginning?'

Dic-Dic did not answer, but wondered just why he hadn't done so himself. He was very grateful when Tembo said, 'When you have other burdens in times to come, do not again cling to monkey wisdom!'

Gogo had his fingers in his Bible. As Daudi finished he said eagerly, 'Goha and I would have been wise to pray for help today. I see it now, for I've been looking

in the Mirror and here it is: "Cast your burden upon the Lord and he will sustain you".'

'And here,' said Elizabeti, ' "Fear not, for I am with you. Don't be afraid, for I am your God. I will strengthen you. Yes, I will help you. Yes, I will hold you up with the right hand of my righteousness".'

'And,' said Liso, 'He says, "Behold, I am with you all the time".'

'Good!' smiled Daudi. 'See how the Bible helps. To strengthen your memories, look at the vaccination scars on your arms. Because they are there you know you are protected from the attacks of smallpox.

'But these scars are only a small signpost to what the Lord Jesus made possible by his cross. By his scars he made a double cure possible for us. He takes away the punishment our sins have earned, also he gives us power and strength both to carry our burdens and to stop sin ruling our lives.'

'Double cure,' mused Gogo. 'This helps me to understand. Why should anyone carry this double burden?'

'Hongo!' said Yuditi, 'I see it too. Surely there is no wisdom, not even a little in following in the way that Dic-Dic took.'

Daudi smiled. 'And also, there is no need.'

* * *

What's Inside the Fable?

Special Message: Give your burdens to the Lord.

Read *Psalm 55:22 and Isaiah 41:10.*

7

SWEET AND SOUR HIPPO

'Many people came to the hospital today,' said Kali. 'I've never seen so many there in one day before,' said Tali.

'Eheh,' said Goha, 'they came because smallpox has attacked their villages and their own families. They have fear and hurry here for help.'

Elizabeti giggled, 'I have never heard so many people so full of words of complaining!'

Goha chuckled and started to mimic, his voice changing with each complaint.

'Ehhh! The heat!'

'Yoh! The flies!'

'Kah! I'm tired of standing!'

'Hongo! Walk all this way to be scratched. It is a thing of no profit.'

'Yoh! I have no joy, not even a little.'

Daudi smiled and sat back on his stool. 'Learn wisdom from these things, and remember, crocodiles kill hundreds, but it is the mosquito bite that kills millions every year.'

'Hongo,' said Dan, crushing one that was feasting on his leg.

'Eheh, and when people say, doing this or that doesn't matter; it is only a little thing, do not believe it. Listen to what happened to Boohoo.'

One day when there were few clouds in the sky Dic-Dic asked Twiga, 'Why does Boohoo, the hippo, walk by himself so much?'

Towards them came Boohoo walking miserably through the bright sunlight. Twiga said quietly, 'He has a way with him that brings small joy to himself or others. Use your eyes and your ears and you'll understand.'

Hippo came up to the animals who were standing in the shade of the great *buyu* tree. 'Oh dear,' he said, 'isn't the sun hot today. It's awful when your skin sun-burns. Most un-com-fort-able.'

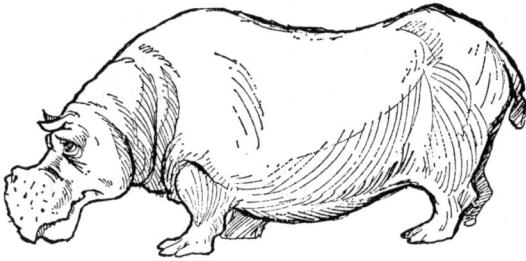

Dic-Dic noticed how sadly the corners of his mouth turned down. Rhino sniffed noisily, and Toto, the monkey, giggled.

'Sen-sit-ive,' mumbled Boohoo, 'That's what I am, sensitive. I wonder why it has to be me who – *er ...*'

'Stop your whingeing!' snorted Rhino, 'stop thinking about yourself. Stop talking about yourself. And better than anything, just stop talking!'

Boohoo shook his head and sighed, '*Er* – you don't understand, really. If your skin blistered when the – *er ...*'

Rhino's eyes were red. He snorted. His great horn prodded aggressively into the air. 'Oh go and jump in the lake you sighing, miserable, skinful of self-pity.' He snorted angrily and strode away.

Boohoo looked after him glumly. '*Er* – you see what I mean? Not what you'd call nice to me – *er* – is he?' He sniffed loudly, 'And I always try to be friend-ly and soc-iable. Always.'

'We're going your way,' said Twiga as he, Toto, Dic-Dic and Punda joined Hippo in his walk.

They moved on quietly until they came near a large patch of thistles. Boohoo's sad voice started again, 'Why don't you say some-thing? I'm doing my best to be com-pan-ion-able, and nobody – er ...'

Toto chuckled, 'Good thing Rhino ran off. Thistles do funny things to his nose.'

A cross, grumpy noise came from somewhere inside Hippo. 'Don't you interr-upt, Monkey. Small Monkeys should – er – be seen and – er – not heard. Er – what was that you said? Thistles? Nasty sort of plant – er – they give me a most unusual feeling in my – er – throat, you know.'

Punda started to grind his teeth, then he kicked up his back legs, hee-hawed and walked slowly away.

'Er,' said Hippo. 'Odd. Not very good at con-ver-sa-tion. I suppose donkeys are like that. I feel it makes the time pass more pleasant-ly if you – er – talk, don't you?'

Dic-Dic's mouth opened to say something, but Twiga shook his head. He knew that while hippos ask questions, they do not want them answered.

Boohoo's voice went rambling on, 'Of course, Punda doesn't have the same trouble as I do with his throat.'

Toto climbed up Twiga's tail, swarmed up his neck, and chortled, 'Awful, if he had been a giraffe and had a sore throat!'

Giraffe's large eyelid winked slowly.

Boohoo sighed, 'Rather dull in this part of the jungle, don't you think? I – *er* – like flowers and things.' He shook his head and plodded stolidly along.

Soon they came to a place where a small stream gurgled down the hill. Ahead were shady umbrella trees covered with yellow blossoms. 'There,' said Twiga, 'that should make you happy.'

Boohoo lifted his heavy head and blinked, 'Oh dear, I can't bear those little yellow flowers. They always make me – *er* – sneeze, and then my nose blocks up, most un-com-fort-able; and itch! – but you wouldn't understand.'

A breeze blew across the river through the umbrella trees. It was cool in their faces. 'Lovely,' said Twiga, 'beautiful cool breeze.'

'Oh,' said Boohoo, 'it will bring the stuff out of those flowers into my nose. I knew it would ...' He stopped. 'Oh dear, I'b going to ...' His flabby sides moved floppily in and out.

Monkey leaped from Giraffe's neck on to Boohoo's head and pushed hard under his nose.

77

'What – er – er, oh dear, hip … hip …'

'Try to stop it,' yelled Monkey. 'I'm helping. Don't sneeze and your nose won't block. Don't sneeze and your skin won't itch. And don't …'

'Oh dear …' gulped Hippo. 'Help! Hip… hip … hip!'

Monkey pushed with all his might. Twiga moved briskly to one side and said to Dic-Dic, 'Get behind that big anthill; when he sneezes he can blow you head over hooves.'

Dic-Dic scampered to safety. He listened to the odd noises that Boohoo was making, and the giggling of Monkey. 'Do you think he's going to sneeze?'

Twiga nodded. 'He would be very unhappy if he didn't. That's the way of hippos.'

Hippo's sides moved like huge bellows. His mouth opened wide. His nostrils quivered. The jungle seemed suddenly silent. 'Hip … hip … hipposhooo!'

Monkey went flying through the air and just managed to clasp Twiga's strong neck. A variety of eyes turned towards Boohoo, who stood there forlornly. 'Oh dear, I'm going to … '

He sneezed again. 'If only you knew how much I suf-fer when I sneeze; my ribs ache for hours and hours and before long my nose gets blogged and by eyes, and itch, oh dear, very trying it is.'

Twice more he sneezed, and then with satisfaction in his voice, he said, 'Dow by dose is blogged broberly. Oh dear. It bakes be so biserable to be like this.'

He wandered off by himself towards the swamp.

Dic-Dic scampered to the very top of the anthill. Here he could talk right into Giraffe's ear. 'Twiga, what can we do for him?'

'If he could think of somebody else for a change, it would do him a lot of good.'

Dic-Dic started to become excited. 'What can we think of?' He jumped up and down, tripped, rolled over and over down the anthill, skidded on the mud of the bank and SPLASH! He was in the fast flowing river.

Away above the curve in the river three pairs of crocodile eyes gleamed and three great bodies slid silently into the water.

'Boohoo!' shouted Twiga, galloping along the river's edge. 'Hey! Boohoo!' He kept his eye on Dic-Dic's small head battling with the current.

Boohoo plodded on. 'Wad's the batter?' he grumbled huskily without turning his head.

Twiga came panting up, 'Quickly, Dic-Dic's fallen into the river!'

'Oh – er – he can swib, can't he? Every-body ought to be able to swib.'

'What chance has he with those crocodiles? Look! See them? Three of the brutes!'

'They wouldn't touch him if I was swibbing with him you know, Twiga.'

'But you aren't!'

'*Er* – yes, that is say, no. I subbose you're right. Oh – *er* – look! *Er* – cub od!'

Boohoo started to run. Faster and faster moved his short fat legs. He plunged through a patch of

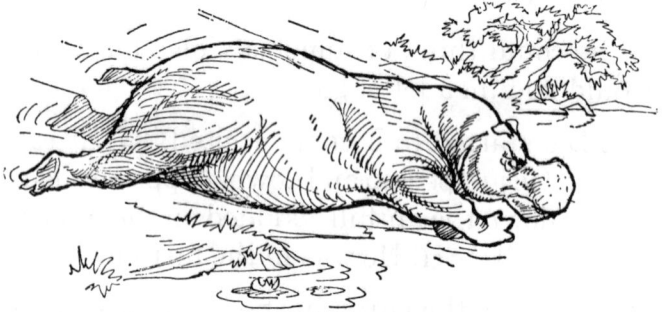

yellow flowers and sneezed and sneezed and sneezed again, but still he hurtled on towards the curve in the river. Then SPLASH! In he went. Swimming strongly under water he came up between little Antelope and the crocodiles. There was a new gleam in his eyes.

'Here I ab, Dic-Dic! I can swib like a fish you know.' He turned his head sharply, 'You, Crocodile! Keep your distance! Keep your distance, or I'll bite you. By aunt once bit a crocodile in half – upset him, it did!' He looked over his shoulder. Dic-Dic was struggling along some way behind. 'Are you all right? Oh, I'b going too fast, ab I? I keep forgetting how well I swib.'

A particularly vicious-looking crocodile surged towards them. Dic-Dic came as close to Hippo's great shoulder as he could, his feet paddling wildly. Boohoo opened his mouth wide and bellowed. The crocodile moved hastily out of range.

Silently the third crocodile swam deep under Boohoo's body. Dic-Dic sensed the danger and spluttered, 'Help!'

Hippo's whole body jerked. There was an odd noise from underneath the water. Boohoo sounded pleased. 'Tried to dive under me he did, but I kicked him in the – *um* – middle. I don't think he liked it at all, do you? Hippos can kick very hard, you know.'

He swam towards the sloping bank. 'Keep near me. We're nearly there now. You'll find your feet on the bottom soon.'

Dic-Dic scrambled out exhausted.

'Good old Boohoo!' cried Twiga and Toto and Punda all together.

Hippo blinked. 'Oh – *er* – what's the matter? *Um.* Oh yes, he'll be all right soon.'

Dic-Dic put his small hooves high up on Boohoo's front shin, and looked up at him. 'Thank you, Boohoo, kind old Boohoo.'

Boohoo blinked, and the corners of his mouth turned up in an odd kind of smile. '*Er* – *um* – that is to say, don't mention it, Dic-Dic.' A puzzled look spread over his face. '*Er* – *um* – did you notice that my nose isn't blocked now? Oh good!'

'Bwana Daudi,' said Gogo, *'we know there is a treatment for smallpox; in your story do I see a medicine for self-pity?'*

From his seat in the wheelbarrow, Gulu lifted himself up. 'Do things for someone else, that is the medicine that stops you thinking about yourself.'

Liso reached out and put her hand on Daudi's arm, 'Also to encourage people and not to fill their ears with your own troubles. This is good medicine.'

A messenger came from the hospital calling Daudi.

'Coming,' he answered.

Gogo walked beside him. 'Thank you for your words today, Great One. I have understood many things.'

'Good,' said Daudi. 'Remember, God never lets his own children suffer for anything unnecessarily. It is all part of his training or his purpose. Sorrow, difficulty, pain – these can do two things to you. They can either make you strong, or you can let them make you sour.'

* * *

What's Inside the Fable?

Special Message: Build each other up in the Lord.

Read *1 Thessalonians 5:11 and Ephesians 4:29.*

8

BAD BARGAIN FOR DUCK

'Hundreds and hundreds of people have been vaccinated,' said Goha. 'Notice anything special about them?'

The children looked at one another. After a pause Gulu spoke.

'None of them caught the sickness?'

Goha nodded vigorously. 'Not a single one. But those who have not been done ...' He shook his head.

'Hongo,' said Yuditi, 'here comes Bwana Daudi. How tired he looks.' She went to meet him. 'Is there much difficulty at the hospital?'

Daudi held up a letter and shook his head. 'This is from Mpesa, from beyond the river.'

'Kah! He is a fundi in the matter of cattle, Bwana.'

'He was,' said the Medical Assistant. 'Listen to his letter: "I will come next week to be vaccinated. First, I have a chance to sell three cows and make a big profit".'

The children sat open-mouthed. 'Did he ... ?'

'Yes,' nodded Daudi. 'Smallpox struck him while he was thinking only of money.'

Daudi sat down. 'Do not let this ever escape from your memory. And to help it stay there, here is the story of Waddle, the duckling.'

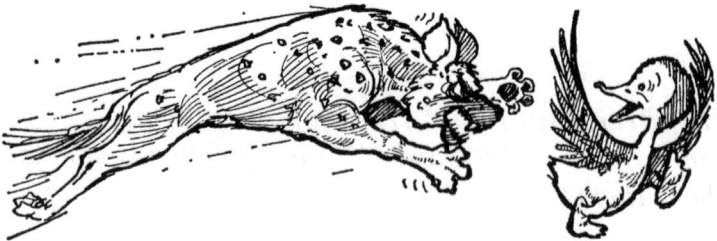

Boohoo the hippo's mouth was full of water lily roots. He tried hard to swallow them. His eyes stuck out. His nostrils grew bigger. But all his voice could produce was a squeaky, '*Er* – look out!'

It wasn't loud enough to reach Waddle, the duckling, and Mbisi, the hyena, was already hurtling through the air towards him.

'Oh dear,' gulped Hippo. 'What a pity. A nice little fellow, too!'

But when Hyena's teeth were only inches from his tail feathers, small Duckling flapped his wings and zoomed gleefully into the air, while Mbisi shot past and landed SPLOSH! Face first in some particularly slimy mud.

Duckling flew happily overhead and quacked, 'Useful things, wings, eh?'

As Hyena shuffled off snarling, Waddle spread his wings and landed smoothly beside Hippo in the

water lily pond, and quacked, 'Thought he'd trapped me, didn't he?'

'Oh – er – yes, and – er – so did I,' agreed Boohoo. 'Nearly choked I did, trying to shout warnings when my mouth was full. Most un-com-fort-able.'

Waddle chuckled. 'One waggle of my wings and he was in the mud. But how I wish ducks had useful feet like hippos. Wonderful help in worm-hunting they'd be.'

Boohoo blinked.

Duckling quacked on, 'I always think hippos are very kind animals.'

Boohoo regarded him with his mouth half open, and then said, 'Er – am-i-able. What do you want me to do?'

Waddle tried to look pathetic and said, 'I'm so hungry, and I like worms better than anything else in all the world.'

'Er, worms?' mumbled Hippo. 'I wouldn't be surprised if water lily roots were more sub-stan-tial. I never – er – eat worms, that is I – um – don't mean to … '

'Would you be very kind to a hungry little duckling and walk along the soft edges of the river?'

'Er,' said Boohoo, 'walk about in the mud? Certainly, Waddle. I – er – like mud. It's sort of soothing to the feet, you know.'

High in the air Vibi, the vulture, circled, his nasty little mind working fast. He watched Boohoo walking slowly and splashily beside the river and Waddle eagerly worm-hunting in his footprints.

Hippo paused in the shade and watched Duckling for a long time until a sad little head looked up at him. 'Only found two, and worms are my favourite food. I like them better than anything in all the world.'

Waddle ran his beak under his wing to clean it and a feather fluttered to the ground. Vibi saw everything that happened. Suddenly he squawked. 'That's the answer! Worms and feathers.'

Vulture swooped down and sidled up to Mbisi with a knowing look in his beady eye. 'Why don't you catch him?'

'Catch him?' snarled Hyena. 'Why don't you catch him, clever! It's his wretched wings that are the trouble.'

Vulture's head moved up and down on his long ugly neck. 'How right you are! Leave him to me. I understand wings.'

Two days later Vibi watched Duckling come glumly along the track from his favourite worming spot, and splash exhausted into Boohoo's water lily pond. 'Not a worm all day,' he quacked sadly, 'not a single, solitary worm to comfort my inner duck.'

A sly voice came out of the shadows. 'Talking of worms, are these the things you mean?'

Duckling's delighted eyes saw a banana leaf full of big juicy worms. He hardly noticed that the leaf was held in Vulture's cruel, sharp claws. Eagerly he quacked, 'Worms! Quick! Give 'em to me!'

'Gently now,' came Vulture's voice. 'You want worms? Here they are. What I need is feathers for a friend of mine. Wing feathers and tail feathers.'

'Simple,' quacked Waddle with both his eyes and all his mind fixed on the banana leaf. 'You give me worms, I'll give you feathers.'

'Right,' rasped Vulture. 'Three worms for a wing feather; four for one from your tail.'

Waddle nodded eagerly and swallowed his first worm.

'Mm, wonderful. Delicious!'

Vibi pulled his first feather. Waddle hardly noticed it or the others that followed. For each worm

tasted better than the last. All the time Vibi's pile of feathers grew but Duckling had no eyes for the changes in his wings and tail.

Some distance away behind an anthill squatted Hyena licking his lips. Seeing that Duckling was interested only in worms, he crept closer and stopped in the shade of what he took to be a great grey boulder.

Ever so gently Vibi plucked feather after feather, while worm after worm disappeared down Waddle's greedy gullet. As he swallowed the last worm Waddle sighed contentedly and rubbed the bulge in front of him with the wing farthest from Vulture. He hardly

noticed that the only feathers he had left on the other wing were small downy ones.

'Lovely,' he murmured, 'delicious worms.'

Hyena strolled out into the sunlight and laughed the sort of laugh that brought out visible goose pimples on poor Waddle. 'Lovely, beautiful worms, *eh!* Lot of good these worms will do you, Duckling!'

Little Duck frantically flapped his wings, but instead of moving up into the air as usually happened, he spun round and round and toppled over.

Mbisi swaggered towards him, his tongue hanging out.

Boohoo had been having a nap in the water lily pond. He opened his eyes and slowly realised what

had happened. 'Oh dear,' he muttered, 'what a pity. You'd have thought he would have rea-lised that – *um.*'

All the time Hyena was coming closer to Waddle. He opened his red moist jaws, 'And now for a ducky little dinner!'

He was just going to bite when the great grey boulder moved forward. 'Oh,' spluttered Boohoo, 'it's Elephant. He – *um* … !'

Tembo's trunk shot out, grabbed Hyena by the tail, and his deep voice said, 'No, you don't!'

With a sudden tug Hyena left all the hair of his tail behind and he and Vulture disappeared fast into the darkest parts of the jungle.

A warm chuckle came from Elephant. He leaned forward, put the tip of his trunk gently under little Duck's bill, 'Are worms as important to you as all that, little Duck?'

Waddle shivered.

Elephant nodded. 'What's the good of having all the worms in all the world if you finish up a dead duck?'

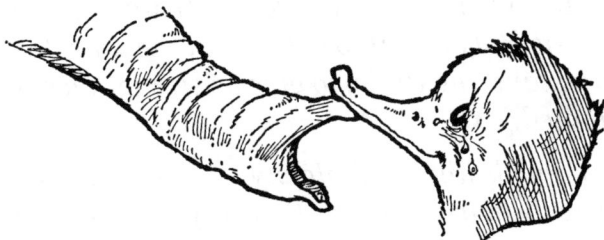

There was a long silence. Then Goha breathed, 'Hongo! That was a near thing!'

Daudi nodded his agreement. 'For Waddle it was worms; for others it can be a variety of things. But remember, in the great Mirror you see the question, "What good will it be for a man if he gains the whole world, yet forfeits his soul?" God wants you to answer that question.'

Again there was a long silence, until Gogo said, 'What did you answer, Bwana Daudi?'

Daudi moved closer to the children. 'I came to Jesus and asked him to forgive me.'

'What did you say, Great One?' asked Tali.

'I prayed, please, Lord Jesus, forgive my sin, please give me everlasting life, and help me to live your way here on earth.'

'Did that work?' queried Kali.

'It certainly did. You see, deep inside me I knew I was trapped by sin. The warning was loud in my ears. My heart and my head told me to decide to ask Jesus to take charge of my life.'

'Kah!' said Gogo, 'it isn't easy to do that.'

'It certainly isn't,' agreed Daudi. 'That is why God gives us his Holy Spirit to help us all the time, to help us understand the Bible, to give us strength when we are tempted.'

Gulu shook his head slowly. 'It isn't easy to say "No" when you want to sin. It is very hard to do what he tells us to do or not to do.'

Daudi nodded. 'But does God expect you to do all this by yourself? Does this burden bend your spine?'

Liso suddenly laughed, 'Also the Bible says he won't test us with more than we can carry.'

Daudi stood up and looked into each face that turned towards him.

'Your soul is more valuable than anything else you own; to know it is safe, is the most important thing in anybody's life.'

There was the sound of Gulu's plaster bumping against the side of the wheelbarrow. 'Yoh!' he said, 'I am glad I heard these words and the warning. My soul is now safe.'

'And mine,' chimed in Liso.

Daudi smiled at him. 'This is wonderful, but you have not reached the end. This is only the beginning. A wise one wrote words which are strong food for your thinking: "The entrance fee to the Kingdom of Heaven is nothing, but the annual subscription is all you've got!"'

* * *

What's Inside the Fable?

Special Message: Don't be tempted by worldly things.

Read: Matthew 16:26 and Romans 8:26

GLOSSARY

JUNGLE DOCTOR'S WORDS AND NAMES
How to say them and what they mean

Animals	*Pronunciation*
Boohoo - hippo	Boohoo
Boko - monkey	Boekoe
Dic-Dic - antelope	Dickdick
Gogo - monkey	Gogo
Goon - baboon	Goon
Hifi - monkey	Heefee
Loon - baboon	Loon
Mbisi - hyena	Mbeesee
Mukamu - monkey	Mookamoo
Tembo - elephant	Temboe
Nyani- monkey	Nyahnee
Punda - donkey	Punda
Soso - monkey	Soso
Toto - monkey	Toetoe
Twiga - giraffe	Twigger
Vibi - vulture	Veebee
Waddle - duckling	Waddle

Names	*Pronunciation*
Baruti	Barootee
Dan	Dan
Daudi	Dhawdee
Elizabeti	Elizabetee
Gogo	Gogoe
Gulu	Gooloo
Kali	Karlee
Kefa	Kefa
Liso	Leesoe
Marita	Mareeta
Tali	Tarlee

Names	Pronunciation
Mpesa	Mpesa
Mwoko	Mwokoe
Goha	Goha
Yuditi	Yoodeetee

Swahili	Pronunciation	English
Buyu	Booyoo	Baobab tree
Bwana	Bwarner	Sir, Mister, Lord
Eheh	Ayhay	Agreement (with nod of head)
Fundi	Fundee	Expert
Hodi	Hodee	May I come in?
Kah	Kah	Exclamation*
Karibu	Kariboo	Come in
Koh	Koe	(As for Kah)
Nyamale	Nyamale	Shut up
Nyamale nye	Nyamale nyee	Shut up all of you
Yoh	Yoe	Exclamation (please raise the eyebrows)

*(tone of voice will indicate amazement, surprise or disgust)

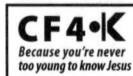